VOICES OF
INSPIRATION

VOICES OF INSPIRATION

Written and Edited by Gerard W. Henry

NEW SPIRIT

BET BOOKS

BET Publications, LLC

NEW SPIRIT BOOKS are published by

BET Publications, LLC
℅ BET BOOKS
One BET Plaza
1900 W Place NE
Washington, DC 20018-1211

ISBN: 1-58314-642-3

First Printing: April 2005

Printed in the United States of America

I would like to dedicate this book to a generation who has enough humility to understand that our present successes and accomplishments are the results of the many sacrifices of those who have gone before us.

ACKNOWLEDGMENTS

I want to acknowledge my grandmother, Savata Henry, who had the faith and courage to leave a small town in North Carolina and establish herself in New York where she became a leading nurse at Lebanon Hospital in the Bronx. As a single mom, she raised a son named Lawrence and instilled in him values of leadership, respect, and integrity. Her son married a beautiful woman named Carol, whose roots were in Louisiana. Carol was the daughter of James and Daisy Messiah, who relocated from New Orleans to seek better opportunities in New York as well. She also received values of leadership, respect, and integrity. Together they have one son who I am honored to be called. Their commitment and unwavering support instilled deep within my soul a determination to be all that God has created me to be and inspire others to do the same. So from the strength and courage my grandparents displayed in seeking a better way, to me being the first in my family to graduate with a Bachelor's degree, the journey continues.

INTRODUCTION

There are many voices on the earth today influencing lives where they have authority. I am a firm believer that the voices we allow to have authority in our lives will ultimately determine our destiny. As Proverbs 23:7 states: "For as he thinketh in his heart, so is he. . . ." Whatever is influencing your thoughts will impact your actions, your habits, and ultimately your destiny. This is why my convictions are rooted in the Holy Bible. I believe the Bible has been written under the divine *inspiration* of God. While some will debate the credibility of the Bible, my response is simply, why would man create a series of sixty-six books written over a fifteen-hundred-year period that ultimately puts that man under eternal judgment? There were more than forty authors ranging from kings, military leaders, peasants, philosophers, fishermen, poets, musicians, scholars, statesmen, and shepherds who contributed. The Bible has been repeatedly verified scientifically with a unified theme. It is more than a fascinating piece of literature that happens to be a best-seller worldwide, but God's authoritative voice on the earth. The Bible is filled with wisdom and insights that anyone who desires to achieve a measure of success in life will find useful.

In light of that, I think we can often miss out on moments when God is speaking to us because we don't read and reflect on Scripture. As a result, we are unable to distinguish when God speaks through another human soul, even if he is not a student of Scripture.

Throughout this book you will be inspired by quotes from many different voices, some of whom have influenced my life directly. I want to encourage you not to rush through this devotional but meditate on each thought for a week. At the end of the day, it is my hope that you will feel more spiritually nourished, encouraged, and determined to become the shining star God has called you to be.

Please enjoy *Voices of Inspiration*.

VOICES OF
INSPIRATION

1

"This world is temporary, eternity is forever; sow your seeds where they truly count."

—Cheryl "Salt" James-Wray
Writer, Speaker, Producer, CEO
GavFam Music

Let us not become weary in doing good, for at the proper time we will reap a harvest if we do not give up. (NIV)—Galatians 6:9

When you are faithful to God over time, you will experience tremendous dividends. Typically the challenge is continuing to persevere during the moments when you want to give up. Some of you are thinking about running away from a trial that God is using to form His nature deep inside of you. DON'T DO IT! The glory of the outcome will overshadow by far the pain you feel right now. And the impact has eternal ramifications. So don't grow weary, my dear soldier. You may be closer to your breakthrough than you think.

Lord, I look to you for strength. Please refresh my soul today. I know I am closer today than I was yesterday in fulfilling my purpose on the earth . . . and I thank you for your promise that in due season I will reap a harvest if I continue to be faithful. Thank you for your faithfulness, Lord. In Jesus' name, amen.

2

"When I die, would it matter that I was even born?"

—Bishop Eddie Long
Senior Pastor
New Birth Missionary Baptist Church
www.newbirth.org

Show me, O Lord, my life's end and the number of my days; let me know how fleeting is my life. (NIV)—Psalms 39:4

It's easy to take life for granted until we encounter death. In many cases it takes funerals or tragedies to cause us to reflect on the reality of life's brevity. How would you spend this week if God said this was your last week on earth? Would your life be a message that will impact generations to come? It will, if you do what God requires of you each day of this week. Jesus said in St. John 4:34, "My nourishment comes from doing the will of God, who sent me, and from finishing His work." (NLT) Let's take on the mind of Christ with a desire to fulfill God's will, not ours, and complete His assignment in our lives.

Lord, I echo Psalms 39:4–5 and ask you to remind me of the brevity of life. Help me to make each day count for you. I know it's not only about what I do, but who I am. Help me to be and do that which makes a difference forever. I love you. In Jesus' name, amen.

3

He will turn the hearts of the fathers to their children, and the hearts of the children to their fathers; or else I will come and strike the land with a curse. (NIV)—Malachi 4:6

The power of a father's words is amazing. My dad shared these words when I was in first grade to motivate me to begin to apply myself academically. At the time, I was clowning around and not taking learning seriously. His words created in me a desire to achieve whatever I set my mind to. This often resulted in me being among the best. I understand that everyone cannot identify with this experience because they may have never known their natural fathers. I do believe that despite the absence of a natural father, there are "fatherlike" voices sent to you that ultimately represent your Heavenly Father.

Lord, I thank you first for being a Heavenly Father who loves me and cares for me. I thank you for your words of affirmation, guidance, discipline, and correction. Thank you for the physical voices you've put in my life to help me develop into the fullness of what you intended. You are an awesome God. Amen.

4

"Fear is the expectation of evil."

—Bruce Haynes
Businessman

There is no fear in love. But perfect love drives out fear, because fear has to do with punishment. The one who fears is not made perfect in love. (NIV)—1 John 4:18

When we are governed by fear, we yield to negative results. Thoughts of death, failure, financial loss, rejection, etc. can prevent us from experiencing many undiscovered blessings that God has planned for us. Although fear can protect us from dangerous situations, I'm referring to a fear that contradicts the promises God has spoken in His word. That kind of fear is nothing short of bondage. Our tendency to be afraid is related to uncertainty about the outcome. Will I arrive safe? What will they say? Will I have enough? Take your eyes off of those people, places, and things and focus them on HIM. The only cure to overcoming your area of fear is by gaining a revelation of God's love for you and the knowledge that He will NEVER abandon you.

Lord, you know my deepest thoughts. I acknowledge that I struggle with fear in the area of _____ and I am asking for a greater revelation of your love for me. Help me to understand that no matter what happens, you are with me and will protect me in every situation and circumstance that you lead me through. Thanks, Lord . . . I love you.

5

"A mind without barriers creates ideas without limitations."

—Rodney Sampson
CEO
The Intellectual Currency Exchange

Now unto Him that is able to do exceeding abundantly above all that we ask or think, according to the power that worketh in us. (KJV)—Ephesians 3:20

Have you ever listened to a young person share big dreams with no clue of what these dreams will require? I think it's interesting how the more knowledge we have about life the more we embrace limitations that prevent us from achieving our dreams. We need to constantly ask ourselves, "If resources were not an issue, what would I be doing with my life right now?" It's God's desire to see what He put inside of you eventually come into being. Remember, whatever you can ask or think, God will do greater as you allow His grace to work in you and through you.

Lord, help me not to limit you by my lack of knowledge and fear. I know that your spirit will lead me and guide me into all truth. So I trust that whatever I am thinking and asking about, you will guide, direct, and do far greater. I trust you and yield. In Jesus' name, amen.

6

"I can take the credit when I mess up, but when I'm good, I gotta give it to God. Because I'm just not that smart!"

—Christopher "Play" Martin
Director/Producer
HP4 Digital Works
www.hp4digitalworks.com

But whatever I am now, it is all because God poured out His special favor on me—and not without results. For I have worked harder than all the other apostles, yet it was not I but God who was working through me by His grace. (NLT)—1 Corinthians 15:10

Whether you can run, speak, negotiate, teach, or bring comfort to those who are hurting around you, the truth is God gave you the gift. There is something that is very natural . . . in fact, almost seamless for you to do because God uniquely wired you with that ability. As we begin to enjoy the blessings that our gifts create we can begin to take the credit for our achievements. I believe, as Chris has stated, the wiser attitude is to recognize that in spite of your special skill, talent, or ability, you must ultimately give honor to the GIVER of your gift.

Lord, I recognize that there are times when I take for granted the gifts you've given me. I thank you for allowing me to bless others with these gifts and will be careful to give you the honor and glory rather than keep it for myself. You are worthy of ALL HONOR, GLORY, and PRAISE, my Lord. Amen.

7

"If we allow the light of God to shine into those hidden places of our lives, we learn that we can stand in the midst of witnesses and not be ashamed."

—Kimberly Rattley
Creative Director
Immanuel Playback Ministries

This is the message He has given us to announce to you: God is light and there is no darkness in Him at all. . . . but if we are living in the light of God's presence, just as Christ is, then we have fellowship with each other, and the blood of Jesus, His Son, cleanses us from every sin. (NIV)—1 John 1:5–7

We all have shameful things in our past that can be used to hinder our effectiveness in being vessels for God. These "unmentionables" can create a sense of shame, unworthiness, and even guilt. This is why some choose to remain in darkness. Light reveals what is really there, both good and bad. If we don't have the courage to face the bad, we will always be haunted by it. It is not until we become comfortable in the light of God's love and forgiveness, that we gain the confidence to live above shame. There is nothing more liberating than to know you are not held captive by your past and when GOD IS FOR YOU, WHO CARES WHO IS AGAINST YOU!

Lord, help me to not hide from you. Those deep, dark places that no one else knows about I present to you. Thank you for your love and forgiveness toward me. Because you believe in me, I can believe in myself. Thank you, Lord. Amen.

8

"Modeling Godly behavior to your children does not guarantee a great result; it just guarantees that they will never be able to point the finger at you for not being the example that they needed."

—Terhea Washington
Owner
September 9 Media & Management
www.thekeynoteaddress.com

But be ye doers of the word, and not hearers only, deceiving your own selves. (KJV)—James 1:22

Anyone who has children or works with children understands the benefits of *following instructions.* Just by the mere fact that you have life experience and have discovered specific consequences associated with specific actions, affords you the ability to speak to a child's life. The problem is if you tell them, "Don't smoke," "Don't steal," "Don't lie," etc. and they see you doing those same things, you are walking in self-deceit. In like manner, spiritual disobedience is essentially not yielding to the instructions of the One who has more than life experience; HE IS LIFE.

Lord, help me not to walk in my own selfish ways, ignoring your words that you've spoken to protect me, prepare me, and prosper me. I don't want to be like a rebellious foolish child, but one who pleases you all the days of my life. Thank you, Lord. Amen.

9

"When obedience becomes your language, overflow becomes your lifestyle."

—Vikki Kennedy-Johnson
President
VGR Entertainment, Inc.
www.eldervikkijohnson.org

For the Lord God is a sun and shield; the Lord bestows favor and honor; no good thing does He withhold from those whose walk is blameless. (NIV)—Psalms 84:11

Do you realize that God wants to overwhelm you with His love? It's true. Like a parent who feels that overwhelming emotion toward his child, God's love is much greater. He will not give us anything that will destroy us or get in between our relationship with Him. Instead, God will consistently give us instructions that will cause us to grow and mature into a place where we can handle all that He intends to release into our lives. So our primary responsibility is to hear and obey. After that, just rejoice for what is to come!

Lord, I thank you for your love for me. I will trust and obey you even when I don't understand everything because I recognize that your plans are to prosper me, not to harm me. Thank you, Lord, for loving me.

10

"Without a vision for the future, you'll always live in the past."

—Reverend A. R. Bernard, Sr.
Pastor
Christian Cultural Center
www.christianculturalcenter.org

As far as I am concerned, God turned into good what you meant for evil. He brought me to the high position I have today so I could save the lives of many people. (NLT)—Genesis 50:20

When I think about Joseph and how his brothers sold him into slavery, I think of a man who overcame much adversity to experience the fulfillment of his dream. He undoubtedly had to work through anger, bitterness, unforgiveness, discouragement, depression, doubt, and more. Yet Joseph overcame it all because he maintained a fear and reverence for God—the giver of his dream. So set aside time to allow the One who knows the end from the beginning to breathe newness of life into you. In His presence you will find the strength, hope, and faith to overcome every obstacle and see your dreams fulfilled like Joseph did.

God, I confess that I am angry, confused, bitter, discouraged (articulate how you feel) concerning the dream you have put in my heart. But in the midst of it all I know you are greater than this circumstance I am facing right now. So I declare that you are great and greatly to be praised. Be magnified and glorified in this situation. In Jesus' name I pray, amen.

11

"I love my husband very much, but no love can compare to the love of Christ."

—CeCe Winans
Artist, CEO
Pure Springs Gospel
www.puresspringsgospel.com

See how very much our heavenly Father loves us, for He allows us to be called His children, and we really are! But the people who belong to this world don't know God, so they don't understand that we are His children. (NLT)—1 John 3:1

Have you ever taken the time to think about how much God *really* loves you? I mean seriously, to think how someone would allow himself to be humiliated, scorned, and tortured so you could experience an intimate relationship with your Creator. This is what Jesus did for Y-O-U! He gave His life as a ransom for yours because that is how valuable you are. I know it can be hard to imagine that God is that passionate about you, but it's true! This is why it boggles my mind when people reject Christ's love and choose to experience life on their own. He has made the way for us to be children of the Living God and experience all of His benefits.

Lord, thank you for loving me despite my faults. I ask that you begin to reveal the length, breadth, depth, and width of your love for me. I recognize this won't always feel good, but ultimately will be for my good. Thank you, Lord.

12

"When your desire to please God becomes greater than your desire to please yourself, your struggle is over."

—Aleathea Dupree
Author of *Though the Vision Tarry: Waiting for My Promised Mate*
www.deepwaters.info

Delight yourself in the Lord, and He will give you the desires of your heart. (NIV)—Psalms 37:4

There is a constant war for your desires. You have to battle with a plethora of images every day to keep your desires focused simply on earthly things. While desiring earthly things is not necessarily bad, the priority must become focusing on making the ways of God your delight. This requires meditating on His words, choosing to be involved in His work, and enjoying private moments of praise and worship with Him. All these things produce a consistent connection with your Creator, who will either affirm your personal desires or alter them. Ultimately, God is after His desires and yours being in agreement. Once this happens, the gates of hell cannot prevail against you.

Lord, I choose to make you my delight this week. Help me to release things that don't really matter to you. I recognize that as I pursue you, I will receive your desires in my heart and experience the abundant life you have planned for me on the earth. Thank you, Lord. You are my delight! I love you.

13

"The greatest work of God that can ever be done is not through you, but in you."

—Fred Lynch
Speaker, Rapper, Producer
Godstyle Productions
www.godstyle.com

I have given you authority to trample on snakes and scorpions and to overcome all the power of the enemy; nothing will harm you. However, do not rejoice that the spirits submit to you, but rejoice that your names are written in heaven. (NIV)—Luke 10:19–20

Do you realize who you become is what will carry over into eternity? I'm not referring to your professional accomplishments. I'm referring to the man or woman of God you develop into. Romans 8:29 tells us that God's will is for us to be conformed into the image of Jesus Christ. How much of Christ's love, joy, peace, patience, kindness, goodness, faithfulness, gentleness, and self-control is evident in your life? None of these things can be attained without Him living inside of you, which is your guarantee to eternal life. As you become like Christ, the fragrance of heaven will be upon everything you do.

Lord, I thank you that my name is written in the book of life. I realize that your desire is for me to look like you and I acknowledge that I cannot do that without you. Live your life through me and make me the person that you want me to be. I yield to you today. Amen!

14

"When God gives the vision, HE is responsible for its completion."

—Bishop Larry Jackson
Senior Pastor
Bethel Outreach International Church
www.frontlinersministries.com

Being confident of this very thing, that he which hath begun a good work in you will perform it until the day of Jesus Christ. (KJV)—Philippians 1:6

When God gives us an assignment it is sooooooo exciting that we can be off to the races! The reality is that when God speaks, the job is much greater than what we can accomplish on our own. As we begin to journey on God's mission for our lives, He has a way of bringing us back to reality. As Psalms 127:1 says, "Unless the Lord builds the house, its builders labor in vain. Unless the Lord watches over the city, the watchmen stand guard in vain." We can sweat and strive to try to make things happen or we can ultimately rest in the knowledge that it is God's responsibility. So don't get frustrated or worried, enjoy the ride and let the pressure be on GOD!

Lord, thank you for the vision you have spoken to my heart. I acknowledge that it is greater than me and rely on you to bring it to pass. Order my steps and help me to recognize your path to bring fulfillment to what you have proclaimed. Thank you, Lord, amen.

15

"Walking in faith is understanding the fact you will literally see the manifestation of the things you speak."

—Audwin Barnes
Evangelist, Senior Partner
Christfirst Clothing
www.christfirstclothing.com

I tell you the truth, if anyone says to this mountain, "Go, throw yourself into the sea," and does not doubt in his heart but believes that what he says will happen, it will be done for him. (NIV)—Mark 11:23

Faith is an integral part of our daily lives and we must not allow anything or anyone to steal our faith. Faith is fueled by God's promises . . . his spoken word. Therefore, any word that is sent to you that is contrary to God's word is an attempt for the enemy to steal your faith. Every day we are unconsciously bombarded with messages, images, and individuals that attempt to invoke fear, discouragement, and unbelief. Our only defense against the onslaught is to feast on God's word and everything associated with Him. I'm not suggesting that you run into your closet and hide out for the rest of your life, but I am saying that time in your closet well spent, will enable you to be effective salt and light on the earth.

Lord, I recognize that my faith is how I exist. Forgive me when I don't feed my faith with your words that bring abundance and life. Help me not get distracted with fiery darts from the evil one that would try to destroy my faith. I confess that my faith will only grow as I feast on your words. Amen.

16

"At some point in life, one is going to be called upon to lead and must respond by action or example. The greatest leadership is by altruistic example!"

—Joseph White
High School Principal
Teaneck High School

Therefore, my dear brothers, stand firm. Let nothing move you. Always give yourselves fully to the work of the Lord, because you know that your labor in the Lord is not in vain. (KJV)—1 Corinthians 15:58

When you have dedicated yourself to a specific mission in life, there are times when discouragement can set in your heart. Thoughts like, "Is this even worth it?" "Who really cares?" "Why should I bother?" "I could make more money doing something else!" can plague your mind. Well, if God is the one who has sent you, then you will never be satisfied doing anything else. Take comfort in the fact that just like Elijah, who thought he was the only prophet left standing for God and was informed that there were 7,000 others who had not bowed their knee to Baal, you are not alone. Because you are an instrument in God's hand, you are making your mark in eternity.

Lord, I look to you for strength. Even in the midst of adversity and discouragement, I will stay the course. I recommit myself fully over to the work you have for me to do and trust that you will fulfill what you desire. My life is in your hands and I wouldn't have it any other way. In Jesus' name, amen.

17

"It's not about talent, it's about the timing of God. You've got the talent, it's about when God is ready to release it in the earth."

—Tonex
Gospel Artist, Producer, Preacher
Nureau Ink
www.yotonex.com

For if you remain silent at this time, relief and deliverance for the Jews will arise from another place, but you and your father's family will perish. And who knows but that you have come to royal position for such a time as this? (NIV)—Esther 4:14

For those of you who are carrying dreams and desires within your heart, wondering if they will ever come to pass, please understand that there is an appointed time. God is just as interested in your journey as He is interested in your destination. It is the actual process that equips you with everything you need to be effective. The process has a way of breaking you down to a level where it is clear to you that the glory that will be revealed in your life is not of yourself. It is usually during your most vulnerable point, when you feel the least qualified, when God says, "Now is the time!" Embrace the process and see His glory.

Lord, I thank you for the talents you have given me. I confess that I get frustrated at times, not understanding why there are not more opportunities for me to express what you put inside of me. Help me to embrace this season, recognizing that you have ordained a "set" time for me to be completely launched into my destiny. Amen.

18

"I'm a husband first, a father second. If I don't romance my wife, someone else will."

—Carlos Diggs
President & CEO
Liquid Earth Entertainment
www.le-eg.com

Husbands, love your wives, just as Christ loved the church and gave himself up for her. (NIV)—Ephesians 5:25

There is nothing more honoring to a wife than to know that she is number one on her husband's list. This can be expressed through phone calls, cards, e-mails, flowers, and many other ways just to let her know she's on his mind. The biggest challenge for husbands who are committed to their families is balancing the demands of providing for their households and attending to the relationship needs of their spouse and children. While this can be difficult, I believe the most important thing is for husbands to pray for their wives. In doing so, God will give insight and direction on how to communicate appreciation and value.

Lord, I thank you for my wife. She is your gift to me even when it hurts. Help me to communicate in special ways how valuable she is to me and release fresh passion in my heart to love her the way you love me. In Jesus' name I pray, amen.

19

"You may not be able to change your family or your church, but you can change yourself through your commitment to consecration."

—Wellington Boone
Founding Bishop
Fellowship of International Churches
www.wellingtonboone.com

I am the Lord your God; consecrate yourselves and be holy, because I am holy. Do not make yourselves unclean by any creature that moves about on the ground. I am the Lord who brought you up out of Egypt to be your God; therefore be holy, because I am holy. (NIV)—Leviticus 11:44

Oftentimes people will try to escape the pain of their circumstances by changing their environment. They may seek a new job, a new relationship, or a new city in which to reside, never recognizing that the adjustment needed is inside of them. God's desire and intent is for us to be like Him. He is holy and will use circumstances to help us change more into His image and likeness if we allow it. So before you look at all the external factors in your life causing you pain, take a moment to examine your heart and see what adjustments God may want you to make.

Lord, I recognize you are holy and have commanded me to be like you. I cannot do this without you and ask that you would help me see where I need to change instead of pointing fingers at others. Whatever you reveal, I will trust and obey. Thank you, Lord. Amen.

20

"God never manifests anything until there is first an environment to sustain it."

—Ralph D. Moore
Trumpeter, Author, Speaker
Sound of the Trumpet Ministry
www.sottm.com

And who would patch an old garment with unshrunk cloth? For the patch shrinks and pulls away from the old cloth, leaving an even bigger hole than before. And no one puts new wine into old wineskins. The old skins would burst from the pressure, spilling the wine and ruining the skins. New wine must be stored in new wineskins. That way both the wine and the wineskins are preserved. (NLT)—Matthew 9:16

When you think about it, any wise investor will not pour his resources into something that would seemingly waste his investment. Oftentimes we think we deserve more than we presently possess. We can even be angry with God because our payday hasn't arrived. Have you ever taken the time to honestly assess what you would do if that moment of blessing did arrive? Perhaps your previous record is an indication of what your future pattern will be. The best action in the present is to make the healthy changes needed to operate at the next level. Do this and observe how God will respond in the days to come.

Lord, I recognize that you desire to bring me into a new season of my life, a season of blessing like never before. Help me to see the adjustments I need to make to prepare for what is to come. I understand that as this new "wineskin" is prepared, you will release new wine into my circumstances. Thank you, Lord, for your wisdom concerning my life. Amen.

21

"Never take yourself too seriously; God has a sense of humor."

—Yolanda Adams
Gospel Artist, Songwriter
www.yolandaadams.org

A cheerful heart is good medicine, but a crushed spirit dries up the bones. (NIV)—Proverbs 17:22

Aren't you grateful for laughter? It's amazing how an amusing moment can break the tension in a room. God has given us laughter to be an emotional lift that can bring healing to a hurting heart. I am convinced that we can have a tendency to major in things that are so minor to God. Even when it seems like all "hell" has broken out against you, God has a unique and creative way of making that situation work for your good. Although the devil thought he had you defeated, discouraged, and dismayed, in God, you will have the last laugh!

Lord, help me to carry your perspective on life's circumstances and never let them see me sweat. Thank you for the gift of laughter. In Jesus' name, amen.

22

"Jesus had no problem with people desiring greatness. He simply taught that true greatness must come through serving others."

—Dean Nelson
National Director
Global Outreach Campus Ministry
www.gocm.org

And whoever desires to be first among you, let him be your slave—just as the Son of Man did not come to be served, but to serve, and to give His life a ransom for many. (NKJV)—Matthew 20:27–28

The terms "servant" and "slave" are not very popular words, especially in the African-American community. Yet this is the posture that is required of every leader who is led by God. We tend to ascend to a position of leadership based on our gifts and strengths. This process of promotion can cause us to carry an attitude of pride whereby we feel the world should revolve around us. Quite the contrary, God has gifted you and allowed you to be promoted in such a way as to help others. The mark of great leadership is how you use your strengths to help those around you to reach their potential.

Lord, I thank you for your example of servant leadership. I realize that you've given me a position of influence at some level. I submit my heart and mind to you so that I may be a vessel who uses my strengths to lift up others instead of seeking to be lifted up.

23

"If a man is not willing to invest in the success of his vision, then no one will be willing to invest in it when he asks this of them."

—Sabrina Guice
Publicist
Guice Media Communications

He becometh poor that dealeth with a slack hand, but the hand of the diligent maketh rich. (KJV)—Proverbs 10:4

I often find that many people want to be rich primarily based on the perceived lifestyle of people with wealth. The "want-to-bees" dream about wealth and riches to escape from the pain of their daily struggles. The "will-to-bees" are determined to pay the price to make the dream a reality. The people who can afford expensive garments, homes, cars, dining, entertainment, etc. typically deserve those privileges because somewhere in their journey they made the necessary sacrifices. They made a decision to diligently pursue their passion and develop their talent. When that decision is made, others will recognize it and come alongside you to see your full potential realized.

Lord, I know you have a plan for my life. Help me to be diligent in the areas that agree with your plan for me. In doing so, even in the process, I will feel like a million dollars. Thank you, amen!

24

"Life is God's gift to us. Service is our gift back to Him."

—Denise Stokes
Motivational Speaker
Denise Stokes, Inc.
www.denisestokes.com

I beseech you therefore, brethren, by the mercies of God, that ye present your bodies a living sacrifice, holy, acceptable unto God, which is your reasonable service. (KJV)—Romans 12:1

Your body is an instrument from which life flows. Your instrument can be used to bring honor or dishonor to your Creator. Of course you will always have a choice of how you use your instrument. You can choose to live for yourself or for God. Just let me remind you that you were born with natural talents, gifts, and abilities. You did not choose them, but they were given to you. Therefore, it is not an unreasonable request that your talents, gifts, and abilities be used in such a manner that bring honor to the One who gave them to you. What is your choice today?

Lord, I don't want to take for granted that I was supposed to see this day and thank you for your grace and mercy. I ask that you help me do my reasonable service this day by loving you with all that I am and loving my neighbor as myself. Thank you, Lord, amen.

25

"If you know who you are in Christ and know the enemy, you will not fear a thousand battles."

—Harry R. Jackson, Jr.
Author, Pastor
Hope Christian Church
www.thehopeconnection.org

Finally, be strong in the Lord and in His mighty power. Put on the full armor of God so that you can take your stand against the devil's schemes. For our struggle is not against flesh and blood, but against the rulers, against the authorities, against the powers of this dark world and against the spiritual forces of evil in the heavenly realms. Therefore put on the full armor of God, so that when the day of evil comes, you may be able to stand your ground, and after you have done everything, to stand. (NIV)—Ephesians 6: 10–13

It would be extremely shortsighted to think that our daily battles in life are simply mere circumstances in the natural realm. While God allows circumstances to develop and mature us, He ultimately desires us to live victorious over them instead of being consumed by them. This only happens as our perspective changes. When we recognize that our battles begin in the unseen realm and then express themselves in the natural realm, we can respond in the same manner. Our ability to confront the unseen realm has everything to do with choosing to be cloaked in God's image first and then we'll see victory in the natural realm.

Lord, I thank you today for Salvation. Because of the blood you shed on Calvary for me I am made righteous. I choose to walk in the truth of your word today, which empowers my faith and peace in you. I will resist the temptation to reflect on thoughts that will be contrary to your word, and decree that I am victorious in Christ Jesus, my Lord. Thank you for victory. Amen.

26

"Christ's sacrifice allowed us to enter a relationship of love and obedience. We must submit our bodies as living sacrifices to His desires. Live in the Spirit, and embrace the lover of your soul."

—Tia Smith
Producer
Talented Sol Productions
www.talentedsol.com

I am crucified with Christ: nevertheless I live; yet not I, but Christ liveth in me; and the life which I now live in the flesh I live by the faith of the Son of God, who loved me, and gave Himself for me. (KJV)—Galatians 2:20

The aforementioned verse is full of wonderful insights to reflect upon. Some would say the Christian walk is extremely difficult, if not impossible, based on the temptations on the earth. This might be true if it wasn't for the power of the cross. Simply said, "If I have enough humility to acknowledge that I cannot live a life of personal holiness, which Christians are commanded to do (Leviticus 20:7, 1 Thessalonians 4:3), then I must totally rely on the One who loved me, and gave himself for me." You see, the power of the cross is me choosing to die to myself or allowing Christ to live in me.

Lord, I will declare your word today as it is written in the King James Version. I myself no longer live, but Lord, you live in me. So I live my life in this earthly body by trusting in the Son of God, who loved me and gave himself for me. I am crucified with Christ. Amen.

27

"When you know better you should do better."

—Kellie Williams
Actress
Hit TV sitcom *Family Matters*

*Teach me what I cannot see; if I have done **wrong**, I will not do so again.* (NIV)—Job 34:32

It goes without saying that we will make mistakes in life. The process of learning and gaining experience in life often happens through mistakes. Unfortunately, not all of us are QUICK learners, and we can find ourselves in the same repetitive cycles that bring harm and hurt to ourselves as well as others. The key to personal growth and development is how quick we seek to find a better way instead of continuing along the destructive path we've been on. Because God loves us, He will reveal when something is wrong in our lives and enable us to change it. Just be wise enough to obey God.

Lord, I ask that you would reveal things in me that I cannot see that need to be changed and give me the courage to receive divine surgery. I know you love me and I know you will help me. I don't want to settle for less than your best. Thank you, Lord, amen.

28

"Your friends bring you joy, but your enemies bring you strength."

—Terri McFaddin
Evangelist, Author
www.terrimcfaddin.org

Dear brothers and sisters, whenever trouble comes your way, let it be an opportunity for joy. For when your faith is tested, your endurance has a chance to grow. (NLT)—James 1:2–3

It is a natural response to want to withdraw from adversity, especially adverse relationships. Sometimes things aren't that simple. Typically we are placed in an adverse scenario to be tested in a specific area in our lives. Will we rise to the occasion and choose the path that reflects the nature of Christ, or will we pursue the path of least resistance? Often when the harder road is traveled, the bumps along the way crack open our outer shell, enabling more of the fragrance of Christ to be released into our lives. God wouldn't have it any other way.

Lord, thank you for every trial and tribulation. I recognize that without resistance there is no growth. I vow that despite the anger, grief, and pain I may experience, I will run to you first and not run away from what you are desiring me to accomplish. You are my resting place. In Jesus' name, amen.

29

"When holding grudges against friends it is not realistic or fair to hold someone captive by an offensive they are unaware they caused you."

—Theresa McFaddin
Speaker, Author of *Supernaturally Attractive*
www.harvestwords.com

If another believer sins against you, go privately and point out the fault. If the other person listens and confesses it, you have won that person back. (NLT)—Matthew 18:15

Forgiveness is a powerful act. Think about moments in your life when you knew you hurt someone and felt extremely bad about it. How did it feel when they forgave you? What a relief, right? Well, maybe someone has offended you and doesn't even realize it. Until the offense is exposed, you are the one truly held captive. Most hurts come from people we care about, respect, or who influence an important aspect of our lives. The issues we struggle with are often related to misunderstandings. So the key is to free yourself. Expose the offense, seek understanding, forgive, and be reconciled.

Lord, I know I am to forgive others as you continuously forgive me but sometimes it can be extremely hard! The hurt I feel in my heart is hindering me from totally releasing that person. I choose to give my hurts to you, trusting you will bring the release in me as I decide to release them. Thank you for the grace to forgive as even I have been forgiven. In Jesus' name, amen.

30

"Your God-given past can empower your God-ordained future."

—Will Ford
Author, Speaker

These were all commended for their faith, yet none of them received what had been promised. God had planned something better for us so that only together with us would they be made perfect. (NIV)—Hebrews 11:39–40

Sometimes we can take for granted the blessings we experience daily. Our present comforts can cause us to forget the struggles of the past that paved our way. When you look at those who have endured wars, economic downfalls, slavery, and imprisonment, you can believe there were some effectual fervent prayers ascending to heaven. I learned a long time ago that part of the blessings that I am experiencing today is related to my personal obedience, but the other part is related to the prayers of those who have gone before me. So be mindful that you are the fulfillment of someone else's prayers.

Lord, I thank you for those who have gone before me, endured and sacrificed so I could have a better life. Let their prayers and works not be in vain. In Jesus' name, amen.

31

"The most powerful things in the world outside of money and things are words . . . what comes out of your mouth can cause you to be successful or unsuccessful."

—Billy Blanks
Creator of Tae Bo
www.billyblanks.com

Death and life are in the power of the tongue, and those who love it will eat its fruit. (NKJV)—Proverbs 18:21

It's so easy to go about our daily lives without recognizing how we are being influenced. All we have to do is take a moment and listen to what we are speaking. The Scripture clearly states that out of the abundance of the heart the mouth speaks. Our words reflect what is going on in our hearts, which reflect who we have been around and what we have been consuming. Getting entangled in the daily grind or rat race can have us in a whirlwind. So we must be careful to take a moment and evaluate whether our words and deeds are producing life or death. The more frequently we evaluate ourselves, the greater certainty we'll have in possessing all that God has ordained for us.

Lord, I recognize that I can get so consumed with the affairs of today that I forget to reflect on what is most important on your agenda. So in the midst of the whirlwind, I submit my mind to you. Influence my thoughts, influence my speech, influence my actions so that I will be pleasing in your sight. I love you, amen.

32

"Looking at the lifestyles of those of us who profess Christ, it's becoming easier and easier to distinguish the true believers from the make believers."

—Lakita Garth
President
Dominion Enterprises, Inc.
www.lakitagarth.com

Not everyone who says to me, "Lord, Lord," will enter the kingdom of heaven, but only he who does the will of my Father who is in heaven. (KJV)—Matthew 7:21

The slave master professed to be Christian. Members of the Ku Klux Klan profess to be Christian. According to the George Barna Research Group, 85 percent of Americans consider themselves to be Christian. Yet, every year wickedness in this nation appears to increase. Unfortunately, we have lost a real sense of who Jesus Christ is and how He desires to live His life through us. What it boils down to is a lifestyle consistent with the nature of Christ. We have to get beyond claiming Christianity from a cultural sense. It has to be more than embracing the traditions of grandma's religion. Now is the time to make a decision whether you are going to become a part of the culture of the kingdom of God.

Lord, I don't want to be among those who honor you with my mouth, but whose heart is far from you. I want my life to be a clear reflection of how you would be on the earth. Do a work of purification in me that I may grow and look more and more like you. In Jesus' name I humbly pray, amen.

33

"The only secret to beauty is knowing how to capture it."

—Elena George
Celebrity Makeup Artist
Hair and Makeup by Elena

Charm is deceptive, and beauty is fleeting; but a woman who fears the Lord is to be praised. (NIV)—Proverbs 31:30

Some people (especially in my industry) base their identity on their appearance. They attempt to meet the physical standards set by popular culture, and forget that beauty is fleeting. Thus, we have plastic surgery and various kinds of makeovers to keep us on the cutting edge of our appearance. If our identity is solely based on how we look then we are extremely vulnerable to being devastated. The key is tapping into the beauty within you. It's amazing how someone who may have some physical blemishes but radiates an inner strength and joy can appear more attractive than the "flawless" fashion model. This inner glow is released to those who choose to reverence God and embrace the truth that they are fearfully and wonderfully made. Be a good steward of what God has given you from the inside out.

Lord, I thank you for my physical attributes. You declare that I am fearfully and wonderfully made. Show me how to be a good steward of this body you have given me and most importantly let the glory of your love shine from deep within my heart. In Jesus' name I pray, amen.

34

"The flow of success begins with a God-inspired vision, leading to a godly process, revealing divine purpose, launching into God-ordained destiny."

—Arthur D. Wright, III, Esq.
Attorney and Counselor
The Wright Law Network

Then the Lord replied: "Write down the revelation and make it plain on tablets so that a herald may run with it. For the revelation awaits an appointed time; it speaks of the end and will not prove false. Though it lingers, wait for it; it will certainly come and will not delay."
(NIV)—Habakkuk 2:2–3

Just as the Virgin Mary was impregnated with the Savior of the world, God wants to plant a seed into the womb of your spirit. This seed is something that will grow and develop as you continuously commune with your Creator. Just be prepared to embrace the process. There will be a season of "morning sickness" as well as times of zeal concerning God's promise. There will be moments of discomfort, loss of sleep, and incredible hunger for more substance to see this seed come to pass. There will be stretching, travail, and eventually delivery. Oh, what a special day that will be . . . so persevere and be amazed at the baby to come!

Lord, I thank you for choosing me to birth a specific vision into the earth. Help me to recognize my role and season as I trust you to bring this vision to pass. Thank you for your faithfulness, even when I'm not. You are awesome, Lord!

35

"Everyone has a dream. If you put God first, He will crown your efforts with success."

—Lucille Hunter
Retired Teacher
Born January 4, 1910

Trust in the Lord with all your heart; do not depend on your own understanding. Seek His will in all you do, and He will direct your paths. (NLT)—Proverbs 3:5–6

Simple wisdom from a woman who has lived nearly a century. Lucille Hunter has impacted a lot of lives teaching in the school system of Louisiana from 1928–1972 (44 years) and has observed the maturation of many. Although the principles in *Proverbs* 3:5–6 are simple, they can be hard to apply. We have a natural inclination to want to lean on our own understanding instead of seeking God's will in all that we do. Yet seeking God makes perfect sense because He knows the end from the beginning. If we seek God first, He will naturally lead us down a path that will ultimately fulfill His plan.

Lord, I know I have a tendency to try to figure things out independent of you which can get me into trouble. Forgive me when I place more trust in myself than I do in seeking your will concerning matters of life. I recommit my ways to you today. Thank you, Lord, amen.

36

"Life sometimes can be like rush hour traffic. All you can do is wait."

—Coy LaSone
Comedian
www.CLasone.com

But let patience have its perfect work, that you may be perfect and complete, lacking nothing. (NKJV)—James 1:4

Isn't it obvious when you need to develop the virtue of patience in your life? It seems like everything takes longer to happen. You drive into an unanticipated traffic jam . . . or get into the wrong line at the check-out counter. You are at your favorite restaurant and everyone's order is ready and served but yours. You are on the phone with someone who takes twenty minutes to communicate a message that only requires two minutes. However, the Lord is working patience in you, His goal is to make your character strong, giving you the capacity to handle anything.

Lord, although I don't like to wait, I thank you for patience having its perfect work in my life. It is apparent that the areas where I'm the least patient are the areas where you want to build my character the most. I receive it, Lord. In Jesus' name, amen.

"Our strength in Christ comes from obedience to the Scriptures, Him shaping our souls, sacrificing our desires for our children, sincerely offering our bodies to each other, and committing all for His will."

—Kevin and Marsha Meredith
Proud parents of Christian, Gabriel, Jonah,
Micah, Benjamin, Hannah,
Rebekah, Sarah, and Hope

For whoever wants to save his life will lose it, but whoever loses his life for me will save it. (NIV)—Luke 9:24

Selflessness or self-centeredness . . . we have to deal with that question daily. Perhaps some of us are not even aware that this is an issue. It is the desire of God for Christ to not just be a part of your life, but to BECOME YOUR LIFE. This can make some of us nervous because of some flaky images of people we've seen who may profess that level of commitment. The truth of the matter is that we are more comfortable with acknowledging Christ as Savior than we are as Lord. Lord infers that we must be in a posture of total submission, which means we surrender our control. Let me ask you, how bad can it be if God is in total control of your life?

Lord Jesus, I ask that you reveal where I stand with you today. Are you just my Savior or have I surrendered to you as Lord? Show me where I need to yield to you more and I will follow. In your name I pray, amen.

38

"To be Christlike is to be revolutionary. I dare to believe transformation is not only possible, it is necessary."

—Dr. Thema Bryant-Davis
Psychologist, Poet, Liturgical Dancer

Therefore go and make disciples of all nations, baptizing them in the name of the Father and of the Son and of the Holy Spirit. (NIV)—Matthew 28:19

The aforementioned verse could only come from the mouth of a revolutionary, whom Jesus is. The concept of disciple-making is archaic in many circles but more contemporary terms are coaching and mentoring. What's unique about disciple-making is that the spiritual disciplines required to be named with Christ are passed down. Too often in the twenty-first century one is left to seek Christian books, tapes, and sermons to experience the transforming power of Jesus Christ. While many people may have had an initial experience or touch from God, Christ's transformational power and presence has not been realized because of a void of disciple-makers.

Lord, you are a revolutionary. Forgive me for staying within my comfort zone and not making an effort to make disciples. Show me whom I am to disciple and who is to disciple me so that I can know you in a greater way and make you known to others. Thank you, Lord, amen.

39

"The beauty of true friendship is that it is a lasting band that God engrafts to one another's heart that remains through the greatest test of time."

—Curtis DePass
Telecommunications Sales Director

Better is open rebuke than hidden love. Wounds from a friend can be trusted, but an enemy multiplies kisses. (NIV)—Proverbs 27:5–6

One important dynamic of your inner circle is obviously having a relationship with voices you can trust. This is easiest among people who love you for who you are instead of for what you do or can do. We need relationships with people who will be honest with us. This will mean we have to listen and embrace things we don't always want to hear. Some things may even be painful, but our comfort is in the knowledge that a friend is speaking to you out of commitment. They will be with you after everyone has gone.

Lord, give me the strength and humility to hear truth when it is spoken. Especially when I don't like it. I also need you to help me strengthen relationships with people who won't be afraid to be honest with me. Thank you for giving me these relationships where I can feel safe in the midst of my own vulnerability. In Jesus' name, amen.

40

"Within the submissive heart of a Godly wife, is a confident wife who understands the power of her influence upon her husband."

—Terry L. Henry
My Wife

Wives, submit to your husbands as to the Lord. For the husband is the head of the wife as Christ is the head of the church, his body, of which He is the Savior. Now as the church submits to Christ, so also wives should submit to their husbands in everything. (NIV)—Ephesians 5:22–24

Now I know some are wondering, "Why'd he go there?" Well, the truth is the word "submission" is in the Bible, but is often misinterpreted and abused. Submission is not a challenge when you are convinced by word and deed that the one in authority loves you. Even when this may not be the case, submission is a principle and practice we all must follow. We struggle with this principle because we don't want to lose our rights. The price is too high to submit myself to another human being who can be just as fickle as the wind, right? That is unless there is a paycheck attached. Seriously, when we choose to submit to those in authority over us, we release God's blessing or judgment to come upon them. Our focus must be keeping the right attitude of heart before the living God.

Lord, help me to have an attitude of submission toward you and to those I am called to submit to. Even when there are disagreements with those whom you have put in authority over my life, help me to communicate with a submissive spirit and not a rebellious one. I love you more than anything and I know you have me covered. In Jesus' name I pray, amen.

41

"Time, money, and knowledge are interchangeable commodities. The combination of any two of these shall produce the other. Nonetheless, knowledge of Christ in the days of youth has even greater value."

—Jonathan Love
Attorney
www.lovelawfirm.com

Wisdom is a shelter as money is a shelter, but the advantage of knowledge is this: that wisdom preserves the life of its possessor. . . . [so] remember your Creator in the days of your youth, before the days of trouble come and years approach when you will say 'I find no pleasure in them.' (NIV)—Ecclesiastes 7:12 and 12:1

While time, money, and knowledge are critical, they can also produce a measure of pride, arrogance, and independence that would persuade one to think he doesn't need God. Instead of trusting spiritual wisdom and insight concerning our practical affairs, some of us have to learn the hard way. The advantage of knowing your Creator, especially in the days of your youth is that you can avoid many unnecessary potholes in life. The treasures within you begin to develop as a result and become a sweet glaze accenting the blessings of time, money, and information you acquire along the way.

Lord, I want to thank you for wisdom today. I ask that this week be filled with wisdom from heaven as I desire to know you more. I know that you can even turn my mistakes from the past into a pathway of blessing, not only to my-self but to others. So I commit to share wisdom, knowledge, and understanding as I receive it from you. In Jesus' name I pray, amen.

42

"I try to stay conscious of the *power* of words."

—LaTanya Richardson Jackson
Actress

So shall my word be that goeth forth out of my mouth: it shall not return unto me void, but it shall accomplish that which I please, and it shall prosper in the thing whereto I sent it. (KJV)—Isaiah 55:11

Words are tremendously powerful. This is why it is imperative that we rely on THE WORD that never fails nor changes instead of the words that often come based on how we feel. If our words are constantly influenced by our feelings we are vulnerable to every storm that comes our way. When we stand on His Word, which never fails, although the winds may blow, and rains may fall, we will not be consumed because our refuge is in His Word. No matter how many disappointments you have experienced in life, please understand it is impossible for God to lie. What He says is true and will be, so align yourself with Him and see what happens.

Lord, I confess there are times when I say things that totally contradict what you say in your Word. I ask that you give me greater understanding of your Word and your ways and that my words will be in agreement with yours. I know if I do so, I will experience victory regardless of the battle. Thank you, Lord. In Jesus' name, amen.

43 "Live for God, but also do the natural. Take care of your body."

—Vanessa Bell Armstrong
Gospel Music Artist

Do you not know that your body is a temple of the Holy Spirit, who is in you, whom you have received from God? You are not your own. (NIV)—1 Corinthians 6:19

Our effectiveness for God is limited to our physical capacity to perform. It has been true in more cases than not in times past that preachers, teachers, evangelists, and the like have died prematurely due to poor health practices. In today's age, where there are pesticides, growth hormones, and other artificial items used on our food supply, we must become more educated and disciplined with our dietary habits. I am grateful that God is a Healer, but I do understand He gives natural wisdom on how I am to steward my body today.

Lord, help me to recognize the limitations of my body, which is your temple. Give me the wisdom and insight of how to care for it through proper rest, diet, and exercise. I don't want to abuse the gift you have given me to experience life on the earth. Thank you for your guidance this week as I present this body back to you. In Jesus' name I pray, amen.

44

"The depth of our relationship with God depends on our willingness to challenge ourselves and persevere through life's obstacles."

—Kenneth M. Mosley
Author, Speaker, CEO
One Focus Communications
www.KennethMosely.com

I want to know Christ and the power of His resurrection and the fellowship of sharing in His sufferings, becoming like Him in His death. (NIV)—Philippians 3:10

Most people are open to know Christ at some level, but few are willing to pay the price for a true relationship with Him. It almost seems glamorous to know Christ in the power of His resurrection yet this doesn't happen without embracing the path of His suffering. Suffering doesn't necessarily mean being tortured, imprisoned, or starved for being a follower of Christ. It simply is a daily dying to ourselves. The mentality of "not my will, but Thy will be done" is where we must live if we want to go deeper with Christ. I'm often amused and amazed how simple obedience, however uncomfortable it may be to my flesh, releases a freshness of life and understanding about my Lord and His ways. So do you really want to know Him?

Lord, help me to declare Philippians 3:10 *with sincerity of heart. I don't want to just recite words, but truly desire in my heart to know you at whatever the cost. In Jesus' name, amen.*

45

"Don't be so consumed with the future that you fail to enjoy the present."

—Richard Dalgetty
Wall Street Executive
Lehman Brothers

Moreover, when God gives any man wealth and possessions, and enables him to enjoy them, to accept his lot and be happy in his work—this is a gift of God. He seldom reflects on the days of his life, because God keeps him occupied with gladness of heart. (NIV)—Ecclesiastes 5:19–20

For those of us who are driven to succeed in life, we can fall prey to the snare of the demands of what we are trying to achieve in the stress and anxiety associated with maintaining your position, the hours required to ascend the corporate ladder, and the relationships sacrificed. This pattern, fueled by a desire to attain a certain status in society, can prevent us from enjoying the blessings of the day. Now, without a doubt, any measure of success and status will come with hard work and diligence. The most important thing is loving what you do. The natural outcome will be success and prosperity. As King Solomon revealed, the gift from God is to be happy with what you do for a living and enjoy the fruit of your labor with loved ones.

Lord, help me not to get ensnared by the cares of this world, chasing after the wind. I do believe if I pursue a livelihood in the area that I love, you will cause me to prosper. Show me how to do this and I will give you all the glory. In Jesus' name I pray, amen.

46

"I've learned that as long as you seek to stay connected with the source—with Him—things *will* get better."

—Patricia Johnson
Minister, Speaker, Author of *Journey Into God's Presence*
Founder, Life Change International
www.lifechangeintl.com

And we know that in all things God works for the good of those who love Him, who have been called according to His purpose. (NIV)—Romans 8:28

Just as we know that seasons change throughout the year, the same is true within life. There is summer, fall, winter, and spring. Each season has its own unique qualities that can be both challenging and refreshing. Because we know a new season is coming, it can be easier for us to endure the discomforts of the present season. We must spend enough time with God so that we can recognize what season we are currently in and also perceive when the next season is coming. So if you happen to be in a winter season of your life today, don't lose heart. Continue to commune with Christ to receive strength and comfort, because spring is on the way!

Lord, I thank you for natural analogies such as the seasons of the year to give me insight into my spiritual life. Help me to recognize which season I am in today and give me the wisdom to effectively prepare for the next season to come. Thank you, Lord, amen.

47

"Faith is like a chair with no legs. God says, 'Sit down' before He tells you that the legs are invisible."

—Andrea R. Williams
President
Tehillah Enterprises
www.tehillahenterprises.com

No eye has seen, no ear has heard, no mind has conceived what God has prepared for those who love Him, but God has revealed it to us by His Spirit. (NIV)—I Corinthians 2:9–10

The unknown can be extremely scary because you have no frame of reference to gauge your expectation. You simply have a word spoken from God that you must trust and obey. The best thing you have going for you is that you know God always has your best interest at heart and will never place you in danger. It is also His tendency to do far beyond what we could have ever imagined as we trust and obey Him. So essentially, you will win in this deal every time. The only requirement is to BELIEVE.

Lord, I recognize that without faith it is IMPOSSIBLE to please you. I thank you as I diligently seek you, I will be rewarded with greater understanding of your ways and enjoy the blessings from your hands. Thank you for putting me in a position to win! In Jesus' name, amen.

48

"For anyone to trust our words, they must first trust our actions."

—Allan Houston
New York Knicks Guard, Entrepreneur
Allan Houston Foundation, H2O Productions
www.allanhouston.com

For if any be a hearer of the word, and not a doer, he is like unto a man beholding his natural face in a glass. (KJV)—James 1:23

Remember the adage, "Actions speak louder than words"? Well if that is true, what are your actions speaking lately? Is it all about you? The strength of what we say comes out of who we are. Our credibility is demonstrated by consistent actions. These actions or activities build a track record that can either harm us or help us. The key is that when we look into the mirror of God's Word, we must remember what is revealed. Our tenderness of heart toward God and our ability to be transformed in his presence will release God's favor toward whomever we need to trust our words.

Lord, help me to be a person of integrity. Reveal areas where my deeds are inconsistent with my words and make me whole. I know as I grow in favor with you, you will give me favor with men. Thanks, Lord! Amen.

49

"Whatever you do, do it so well that no one can do it any better."

—John Harrison Warrick, Sr.

Whatever you do, work with all your heart, as working for the Lord, not for man. (NIV)—Colossians 3:23

A country boy, one of eleven children from Baxley, Georgia, John Warrick, Sr. went to Georgia State College to learn brick masonry. He could not join the union or get big jobs with big companies because he was black. He worked for the WPA, did small jobs for people, and made flower-pots to help support his family. Later in life, he taught masonry at Georgia State College, which is now Savannah State University. John Warrick died at the age of sixty from injuries caused by an automobile accident—and after being in a coma for eleven days. He worked so hard over the years, he had no fingerprints left on his fingers. They are imprinted on his daughter's heart, Jean Elizabeth Warrick Toomer, a graduate of Howard University.

Lord, help me to work in a way that honors you. Let my fellow colleagues be drawn to who you are by my work ethic. Thank you, Lord. In Jesus' name, amen.

50

I have come to realize that the two thousand promises of God to me as His child are not automatic. I must exercise the principles of God in order to experience the manifestation of God's promises."

—Ralph LeBlanc
President
PetroSavers National Corporation
www.petrosavers.com

A faithful man shall abound with blessings; but he that maketh haste to be rich shall not be innocent. (KJV)—Proverbs 28:20

There's a stability reflected in someone who can be called faithful. If a request is made to this person, he will accomplish the task. If he is asked to be somewhere, he will be on time. Stability and dependability are strong attributes that are only proven over time. A person's consistent performance creates the credibility and confidence that they can handle more. Of course God will release more to these individuals. So it should not be a surprise that one who is faithful will abound in blessings.

Lord, I want to be among the faithful. I realize this is demonstrated over time. I commit myself anew today to be faithful to your word and your people. I can't do this without your grace. Thank you, Lord. In Jesus' name, amen.

51

"You lose the right to complain about that which you tolerate."

—Terry Wayne Millender
Founder/CEO
Gospel Invasions Worldwide
www.gospelinvasions.org

This day I call heaven and earth as witnesses against you that I have set before you life and death, blessings and curses. Now choose life, so that you and your children may live. (NIV)—Deuteronomy 30:19

Faith and conviction are not passive but active. You cannot say you have faith in Christ and not express his views concerning matters in today's society. When Jesus walked the earth, he influenced the environment wherever he went. His disciples actually thought that he had come to overthrow the governing systems of their day. On the contrary, Jesus came to establish His kingdom in the hearts of men. As His ambassadors, we are to do the same. Christ is literally depending on you to be His eyes, ears, mouth, and feet on the earth. The idea of choosing life over death is simply making a decision to experience the reality of God's kingdom in every area of our lives.

Lord, I choose life today. I know you are the Giver of Life and if I follow your ways, I will experience life abundantly. I choose Life. Amen!

52

"Your purpose is something you love to do, are good at doing, and honors God while blessing others."

—Carl Jeffrey Wright
President and CEO
Urban Ministries, Inc.
www.urbanministries.com

For we are God's workmanship, created in Christ Jesus to do good works, which God prepared in advance for us to do. (NIV)—Ephesians 2:10

Sometimes we can make things more complicated than they need to be. If God has placed a passion inside of you (something you love to do) and given you a talent to do it (something you are good at), then why would His purpose for your life operate in a totally unrelated area? Some of us labor over the question, "What is my purpose here on the earth?" not recognizing that the Lord already wired us from within our mother's womb to fulfill His assignment on the earth. Because the Lord wired us, it is only in HIM that these things can be fully realized. But as the above-referenced Scripture clearly states, God had already prepared good works for us to do in Christ Jesus. It is apart from Christ that we can do nothing.

Lord, I thank you for the good works you have preordained for me to do. I understand that only those things I do for you will have an eternal impact. That is my desire. Please reveal to me the doors I must walk through to enter into the fullness of why you created me to be on the earth. Thank you, Lord. In Jesus' name, amen.

53

"When I have had a really rough day, or have felt discouraged for whatever reason, I have always found comfort in knowing that the Lord walks with and keeps me daily."

—Tara Griggs-Magee
Executive Vice President
Gospel & Urban Music
Sony Music Entertainment

The Lord is my shepherd; I have everything I need. He lets me rest in green meadows; He leads me beside peaceful streams. He renews my strength. He guides me along right paths, bringing honor to His name. (NLT)—Psalms 23:1–3

What comfort it is in knowing that "Even though I walk through the valley of the shadow of death, I will fear no evil, for you are with me; your rod and your staff, they comfort me." (Psalms 23:4) In spite of the challenges a day may bring, the Lord said we could be of "good cheer" because He has overcome every one of those challenges. So we can go to Him to find rest and refuge. He is faithful not to lead us or allow us to stray too far from the herd. We just can't ignore His staff that brings comfort and protection.

Lord, I agree that you are my shepherd. You care for me, protect me, guide me, never leave me, or forsake me. Thank you, Lord. Amen.

54

"What if Moses would've done what Noah did? Never get caught up in a system that works, without hearing God."

—Tye Tribbett
Musician, Writer, Producer
www.tyetribbett.com

But Samuel replied: "Does the Lord delight in burnt offerings and sacrifices as much as in obeying the voice of the Lord? To obey is better than sacrifice, and to heed is better than the fat of rams." (NIV)—1 Samuel 15:22

Moses was a great man, who endured a lot in leading his people out of Egypt toward the promised land. Unfortunately, Moses never entered into the promised land because he never got control over his greatest character flaw—anger. It was his angry act of disobedience that prevented him from enjoying the land flowing with milk and honey (Numbers 20:2-12). Conversely, Noah was able to press through the sneering voices of his day and obey God's word. The result was deliverance for him and his household, with Noah ultimately becoming the heir of righteousness that comes by faith (Hebrews 11:7). When we refuse to deal with deep character issues that God wants to change, we make ourselves vulnerable to becoming disqualified from experiencing the fullness of what God has intended for our lives.

Lord, I do not want to be disqualified from experiencing all that you've planned for me. Open my ears to hear your voice and I will choose to obey your Word . . . even when it hurts. In Jesus' name, amen.

55

"In the western culture the true definition of humility has been lost in the era of 'bling-bling,' but the heart of God is closer to those who have chosen the path that lacks the paparazzi."

—Kirk Franklin
Writer, Producer, Gospel Music Artist
www.nunation.com

Young men, in the same way be submissive to those who are older. All of you, clothe yourselves with humility toward one another, because God opposes the proud but gives grace to the humble. (NIV)—1 Peter 5:5

We undoubtedly live in an age of materialism where if we are not careful, our sense of self-worth will be associated with things we possess. We will continuously strive for more things in an effort to communicate that WE ARE SOMEBODY! In some instances, the pursuit for nice clothes, nice cars, nice homes, etc. is really a cry for love and acceptance. When you know who you are, you don't have to prove it. Nor do you have to try to build yourself up to feel better than the next person. The truth is all of those things can be lost in a twinkle of an eye. God is not opposed to wealth. He is opposed to pride. We must use the resources God has given us to serve others. If we don't, the wealth we receive will have many sorrows with it. (Proverbs 10:22)

Lord, help me to stay focused on the essentials in life—loving you with all my heart and loving my neighbor as myself. I don't want to be in opposition to you, so show me where I must humble myself that I may experience more of your grace to become the treasure you've ordained me to be. In Jesus' name, amen.

CONTRIBUTORS

1. Cheryl Salt James-Wray
2. Bishop Eddie Long
3. Lawrence W. Henry
4. Bruce Haynes
5. Rodney Sampson
6. Christopher "Play" Martin
7. Kimberly Rattley
8. Terhea Washington
9. Vikki Kennedy-Johnson
10. Reverend A. R. Bernard
11. CeCe Winans
12. Aleathea Dupree
13. Fred Lynch
14. Bishop Larry Jackson
15. Audwin Barnes
16. Joseph White
17. Tonex
18. Carlos Diggs
19. Wellington Boone
20. Ralph D. Moore
21. Yolanda Adams
22. Dean Nelson
23. Sabrina Guice
24. Denise Stokes
25. Harry R. Jackson, Jr.
26. Tia Smith
27. Kellie Williams
28. Terri McFaddin
29. Theresa McFaddin
30. Will Ford
31. Billy Blanks
32. Lakita Garth
33. Elena George
34. Arthur D. Wright, III, Esq.

35. Lucille Hunter
36. Coy LaSone
37. Kevin and Marsha Meredith
38. Dr. Thema Bryant-Davis
39. Curtis DePass
40. Terry L. Henry
41. Jonathan Love
42. LaTanya Richardson Jackson
43. Vanessa Bell Armstrong
44. Kenneth M. Mosley
45. Richard Dalgetty
46. Patricia Johnson
47. Andrea R. Williams
48. Allan Houston
49. John Harrison Warrick, Sr.
50. Ralph LeBlanc
51. Terry Wayne Millender
52. Carl Jeffrey Wright
53. Tara Griggs-Magee
54. Tye Tribbett
55. Kirk Franklin